# SADNESS BELONGS TO THE UNIVERSE

KLEANDROVA HANNA

# SADNESS BELONGS TO THE UNIVERSE

*This is a work of fiction. All of the characters, names, incidents, organizations, and dialogue in this novel are either the products of the author's imagination or are used fictitiously.*

*iUniverse books may be ordered through booksellers or by contacting:*

*iUniverse*
*1663 Liberty Drive*
*Bloomington, IN 47403*
*www.iuniverse.com*
*844-349-9409*

*ISBN: 978-1-6632-2747-8 (sc)*
*ISBN: 978-1-6632-2749-2 (hc)*
*ISBN: 978-1-6632-2748-5 (e)*

*Library of Congress Control Number: 2021919230*

*Print information available on the last page.*

*iUniverse rev. date: 09/16/2021*

# CONTENTS

# PART 1

# WILFRED

There was a place where I would go whenever I felt lost or desperate. I didn't find this place myself—my sister did, and she showed me how to get there. She called it "the island." And indeed, it looked like an island to her. A wide beach of black sand and a dark ocean before my sister's pleased face. The air was fresh and salty there, so her head was light and her worries disappeared. The Northern Lights appeared above my sister's head like a crown each time she turned to the north.

That was exactly how my sister described the island. Had I ever been to the island? Yes. Had I ever seen any of this for myself? No. And to be completely honest, I often wondered how it was even possible.

The answer to this riddle was that this place, which I knew as "the island," sensed what you needed and gave it to you in a way you could not possibly achieve by yourself. The island could *shape* the missing puzzle and complete you. Inside and out.

I always went to the island alone, but I never felt lonely there. There were no thoughts and therefore no doubts. I would think and I would do. I would do whatever I thought. I experienced an amazing feeling of being welcomed by this place. I had unlimited power in this place, and I was unlimited in myself. I was carrying the heart of the island and it felt right. No, I *was* the heart of the island. I could truly say there was no other place like it. The island was *the one.*

My sister and I could go there at the same time, but we would never meet. The island would not let that happen. It also would not let you stay there for a moment longer than you need.

"*Wake up!*" I told myself as I came back to our shared reality. I was complete, full of life and balanced. I always left the island feeling that way.

I remember the day the island let me become a part of it. I was walking through a crowd of people on the main square in Beijing. It was spring—the city was always spectacular at that time of the year. Sadly, I was so distracted by my thoughts that I hardly noticed the changing of the seasons.

I had just reached the edge of sanity. I stopped in the middle of Tiananmen Square and gazed down at my hands. They did not look familiar to me.

It was all inside. Imagine a planet dying. It moans before it finally splits apart, crushed by some invisible power, and there is no sound to any it. None. I was deaf to its moans, but all the pain, like a huge concrete wall, was pushing against my chest until it reached somewhere deep under my ribs.

A few people looked at me with concern as they passed, but they didn't stop. It was close to 9 o'clock in the morning and they were in a hurry to get to work on time.

A woman in a white coat stood watching me. I could have sworn she was looking right through my face and deep down into the darkness.

She waited until I noticed her interest, and after I did, she walked directly toward me. Her face did not betray any particular emotion. She looked calm—the same way people look when they have nothing to lose or nothing to be afraid of. They are free and confident because they are not attached to anything, but also apathetic because for the same reason.

"Let me help you," she said, slipping off her glove.

The skin of her palm was red. It was not infected and it had no wounds. It was just a perfect shade of red.

A thought came to my mind. *"Too much energy floating in her tiny body. That is why her palms are red."*

The moment she made contact my hand, I lost touch with everything around me. I could not say for sure if I left Beijing or if Beijing simply ceased to exist. The street and people disappeared. I disappeared myself, as well as my inner pain. The woman who relieved it turned out to be a guide. Without her, I would never have entered the island.

There is no record of it. It has no location. No road can bring you there, and no jet can fly toward it. The island cannot be found by anything or anyone until it *decides* it wants to be found. And that day, it decided it wanted to be found by me.

After some time on the island, we came back to Beijing. We returned to the very same spot, as though we had never left. There is a difference in time between here and the island. It feels like you have been there for hours, but when you get back, you find yourself in the exact moment you left.

My body felt heavy and clumsy, like I hadn't used it for days.

"Dizzy? That's because it's your first time. It feels like you've got extra pounds and your body doesn't fit anymore, right?" she smiled.

"Exactly!" I responded with excitement.

Of the long list of questions I was about to ask, the main one was why, among all of the people on the street, she chose me.

"With all due respect, I would never choose you," she responded. I liked her joke.

"The island told me to get you," she said.

I asked how she found the island for the first time and managed to enter.

"I doubt we can do it by ourselves. I got an invitation," she said. "Let's have a drink and I'll explain everything."

I nodded and looked around.

"The weather is the same as when we left."
"Everything is the same, except you."

Later, in a nearby restaurant, she told me that my real name was Wilfred, and from now on, she was going to call me that. She never told me her name, so I simply called her "sister." She told me that the island had not communicated with her directly until today.

It sent her the image, a simple thought of me standing in the main square in the capital of China.

"And what happens now? Are there any side effects of entering this place?" I asked.

"None," she said, quickly glancing down at her gloves and then back at me. "From now on, just live your life and come to the island from time to time." "And if I don't want ..." I started.

"Then don't. No one is making you do anything," she said.

After a little more conversation between us, she got up to leave. I tried to stop her. I still had questions to be answered, but she made it clear that there was nothing to worry about. And she was right.

A year passed since my first meeting with my sister. In that time, I had gained an incredible sense of calm, which was the result of my short trips to the island. I became balanced and confident about everything and everyone. There were few things that had any real influence on my inner state. After all, I was just a man, but most of the time, I felt blessed. Blessed *how?* Not like a pop star, but in the way I imagined Buddha would feel.

Times in my life when I suffered from emotional swings and constant overwhelming destruction now felt as distant as the Middle Ages to me. They were gone from my mind.

By this time, my sister had stopped coming to the island. She did not explain why. At her birthday party, she cornered me in the hallway for a quiet moment.

"I am not going there anymore," she said, passing me a second piece of cake. We never talked about it again. And there was nothing to talk about. Two months after her birthday, she also stopped showing up in my life. We had no quarrel or bad feeling between us. I was simply told that she was going to be away, so everything seemed normal.

There was only one thing that puzzled me for a while. From our first meeting that morning in Tiananmen Square to the last time we saw each other, her gloves changed from short wrist-length ones to a type that almost reached her elbows. And she never took them off in front of me or anyone else. The last time we met, she looked sad. She tried to persuade me that it was simply calmness, not sadness, but I can distinguish one from the other. Something was bothering her, and she chose not to share it with me.

Back when we were particularly close, she always insisted on me focusing on *now*, and I trusted her on this matter. Despite my trips to the island, I still had a life to lead. Soon, I found what I was good at, and I eventually became a professional in that field. I became an engineer obsessed with tunnels, especially their varieties in the solar system and far across its conventional borders.

All summer, I worked on a huge, promising project. The concept of the tunnel as we know it was about to change inevitably and forever. I spent most of my time working on it, dedicating my energy to my intellectual child. On one hot August day, I finally identified what I was missing, and I could not ask for more. There's a blessing behind the ability to recognize what you need in time. And needless to say, I am blessed.

After a lot of hard work and being just a step or two away from my goal of being an accomplished engineer, there was one thing I had to do without delay. I had to step back.

I had to set my overworked brain free from the burden it had been dealing with and take a fresh look at the project later.

I was planning to leave my studio for a while. I needed fresh air somewhere in the south of the country, where I already had things to do. I stepped back to have a final look. Each touch of my fingers could turn the digital picture before me to the left or to the right. With my index finger, I could turn it over. I zoomed in on one particular part, investigating it without any expectation of finding something new. All of the changes I made on my board were completed in real time on a higher level. I checked the other projects that I had already completed. I was satisfied with what I saw, but I knew I could do better. The level I was eager to reach was hardly attainable in one lifetime, until one day, I simply decided I could do it.

A comforting feeling filled in the room. I sensed it like an animal can sense the coming rain. My beloved Rose was almost here, so I turned my head toward the door, waiting for her to appear. A second later, a woman in a light summer dress entered the room carrying a tray with two cups of coffee, spoons and a small bowl of nuts.

I watched how she gracefully walked to the table, then carefully placed the tray down and took one cup in her hand. I was fascinated by the way she moved. I stepped closer and touched her skin. I wanted her to know that I was there, but I wanted too much.

I called her Rose, and I had no memories of my existence without her. I did not underestimate how easy it was to lose myself, and Rose was my proof that I was still sane. No matter how hard life got, she was always there to point me north. We consciously kept a distance of one step between us, because if we got any closer to each other, we would emerge. That was how things were for us until this incarnation. However, this time differs from any other in the most unpredictable way. The woman who was now drinking coffee before me was a reflection of my real Rose. She was her shadow. The real creature I was so connected to was lost during the transition.

How could I let that happen? How could I deal with it? I could not. That was why, even in all of my previous lives, I had no memory of the one where it happened. No thoughts or images reached my mind from that time. My memories were blocked so I could move on from the loss I had suffered. One of which was my Rose. I came to Earth first, and I did not find her anywhere, so I waited. When I realized she was not going to come by herself, I immediately started my search for a suitable body for her. It took time that I did not have. I got the body, but she never fully came back.

Rose looked at my creating board.

"It looks like a wormhole!" she announced.

From time to time, she came back to me. She could hear what I said and even answer me with a phrase or touch, but she appears and fades like the changing of the tides.

"You are right. It is a wormhole," I said, going to the table to take a cup for myself. "This project is a tunnel, like the one that goes through a black hole and leads to another part of the universe. Can you imagine if your destination was so far away that it could not be reached in a lifetime, but be using this tunnel, you would get there in … an hour?" I said.

"Interesting." She took another sip of coffee. "These tunnels, as far as I know, were forbidden. They are …"

"…unstable, I know. Gravity is always trying to cut us away." I responded. Although it seemed like we were having a conversation, she was not answering the questions and did not follow the pace of it.

The coffee she made turned out to be as good as I could hope for. My face looked pleased and I hoped she would notice it.

"It's difficult to establish connection, and it's even more difficult to keep it stable. Anything could go wrong at any second, so corporations refused all solutions that involved the human body. It's too fragile for such a journey," I added.

"Ouch!" The coffee was still hot, and she was drinking it too fast.

"Careful. Actually, yes, that's what I am talking about," I said.

"What are you doing right now?" she asked. Her mind was far away, watching me write a letter in one of our past lives. But I would answer her now and keep up with our current conversation, simply because she was here and her presence comforted me.

"Good question. I am looking for a way to stabilize the tunnel. Before, I believed that exotic matter would heal my headache. It has negative mass. It does not obey the laws of gravity, so when gravity is trying to close the tunnel, cutting it off, the exotic matter will not let that happen. Instead, it tries to open it," I said.

I watch her beautiful face closely. In each incarnation, I was obsessed with her cheeks and forehead. Some things never change.

"Ask me if I can keep it stable for a period of time." I said. I needed it to be asked precisely by her.

"Can you keep it stable for a period of time?" she asked.

"It is possible but also dangerous. Come here," I said as I swiped down to show her my other project.

"The tunnel that you see right here is different. It is not about traveling through space; it is about traveling in another reality. That's the future of engineering. Pay attention to the upcoming part. I know what I am missing and, most importantly, I know it exists. In this reality, here and now. I could not ask for anything more. All I need now is to find it before any other engineers get to it," I said.

"No one knows about your work," she said.

"Yes, but thoughts can get into anyone's head. If they shoot into an engineer's mind, I will have a competitor."

I suddenly smiled. I was almost certain she would like to wish me good luck, so I just said, "My job has nothing to do with luck."

"I hope you are fast and exact in what you intend to do," she replied. She heard me and answered on time.

"That's exactly what I need."

I move closer to kiss her cheek. Twice. After all, it's never enough.

My life consisted of three main components: my job, my Rose and trips to the island. All three were irreplaceable and relatively stable until Anna appeared in my life.

She called herself Anna, which was not her name. She could call herself anything she wanted, and we did not mind. What mattered was that she was just like us, an ancient soul, one of the first who was granted by the flesh.

Rose and I discovered Anna at the end of her circle. This is her last time on Earth, which meant she experienced the constant pressure of grief, the roots of which reached too far. She was too close to the end, so nothing particularly mattered to her.

Three months after we met, Rose and I were ready to move in with Anna. We did not know how to do it without causing any trouble for both sides. In the end, it happened almost naturally.

We invited our new friend to spend a weekend with us. We planned to drive to a small village not far from Beijing, where we could climb a mountain and visit an old Buddhist temple. We did what we planned, but on the way back, something impossible these days took place: we got lost.

The road we chose did not lead us to our destination, but rather away from it. We kept moving, and soon after sunset, we arrived at a private area. Anna was walking slightly behind Rose and me. She did not care where we were until she saw a completely white wall. The moment her eyes reached the construction, she went ahead to have a better look at it. Her tall figure stood before the chamber, a child born out of an alliance between futurism and an architect with broken but healed heart. The house was a manifestation of space, simplicity and light.

"I want this house," Anna said aloud and magic began.

Soon, the owner came out. When he noticed how Anna was staring at his house, he came closer to ask if we were lost and needed help.

"I don't need help," Anna answered. "I want this house."

She repeated her statement confidently, and the way she said it was more persuasive than any demand. It was a decision.

Rose and I watched how the man's face changed when he heard what she said. We did not understand what was going on, but over the next three days, we gradually moved in.

Later on, Anna explained that day to us in her own unique way.

"The previous owner decided to give us his house
because we are nice people," she said simply.

I laughed for a minute straight. We were indeed nice people,
but that was not a good reason to give us a house. Anna was the
reason. She could get anything by just pointing at it because her
decision was the law in this reality. The closer she was to the end
of her circle, the more powerful and indifferent she became. She
was incredibly gifted, but since she was sad most of the time, it
was neither a gift nor a curse to her.

Just as I would not boast about my ability to read, Anna never
spoke about her gifts until they occasionally appeared in our
everyday lives. One of these gifts was her extreme attractiveness,
which made her irresistible to basically everyone. Men and women
were eager to express their feelings to Anna, and most of the time,
they did it in unhealthy and abundant ways. Our shared house
stood on the breach of this affection.

Everyone had his or her own unique way to surrender. From
roses to threads, it was all the same.

All of them wanted to be sure that whatever they gave was
accepted. This was how they knew Anna belonged to them.
Anything more profound, like Anna's attraction in return, would
simply destroy their mental health.

Rose and I had just got back from the grocery store. The
moment I approached the entrance door, I knew someone was
inside. A stranger who was, most likely, already far away, but he
or she had left an emotional trace.

I told Rose to stay outside and wait for me to come back. As I entered the house, the floor of the hallway was covered with roses. Without taking off my shoes, I walked directly to Anna's bedroom. There was a gift box on the bed. It was nicely wrapped and carefully put in the place where Anna felt most vulnerable. The ribbon and tag had something to say: "Eat me." I tore the wrapping paper and opened the box.

It was a heart. It was pumping the blood of an animal once, and now I was touching it with my hand. I put the heart back into the box and sighed. Accidents like this one had happened before and I knew they would happen again.

"Wilfred!" Rose called. I left the bedroom and descended the stairs.

"I am here. Nothing to worry about. One of Anna's admirers made a visit."

"What is it this time? Flowers or curses on the walls?" She joked, passing me one of the paper grocery bags filled with cauliflower.

"Both," I said.

After everything was cleaned in the kitchen, we were ready to start cooking. It was my turn to cook, and I was in a hurry to get started because Anna always arrived on time.

Two more months passed before another of Anna's abilities showed up. She started talking about the past, which led me to the conclusion that she was haunted by it. It was eager to be received and understood. The past does not exist anymore, but its influence on Anna was real.

I was never very concerned about her condition until I realized that the past she was haunted by was my own. Anna was an active reader of my past lives. It was like reading a book written in a language you do not speak. But in my case, there was no need to understand the language since the book was full of bright pictures.

While cutting greens in the kitchen and talking about her day, she could suddenly start describing the clothes I wore on a battlefield. I liked to listen to my own lives from her perspective. She also was fine with it until one morning, she discovered something that frightened her.

That day, I woke up unusually early. Rose was still sleeping, so I quietly left our bedroom. I got to the kitchen, where I found Anna working on her creating board. She started studying architecture a week ago, and we supported her as much as we could. However, her new interest was destined to fade in a matter of a month or so. Maybe sooner. Nothing could ever keep her involved for longer than that.

Anna had been working all night, but she didn't look tired. When I entered the kitchen, she looked up at me.

"You woke up just in time. I've found the day when it happened, with you and Rose. On that day, she is still herself," she said.

I had told Anna the truth. That I had no memories of that time, but my words only encouraged her to talk about it.

"There was a tunnel," Anna said, putting down her work to focus on me. "It is the biggest I've ever seen. And you were about to get through it."

"That means I have been interested in tunnels for a while," I smiled.

"In a way," she agreed, closing her board, getting ready to tell me more.

My past comes to her often, and when that happens, she can't be quiet. If she doesn't speak up, it will haunt her until she finally does. I have no choice but to listen all the way to the end. And as a general rule, I was doing it on my own terms.

I took two cups out of the cupboard.

"I'm going to brew some coffee. You have until I put your cup in front of you to finish. Deal?" I asked.

"Deal." She closed her eyes and got ready.

She needed some time to concentrate on the particular date, so I did not disturb her until she began to speak.

"I cannot see you or Rose, but I know both of you
are present. You are both very close to the tunnel.
Wait ..."

Her face instantly changed, as if she saw something unpleasant.

"You are not going there by yourself. It pulls you.
The tunnel pulls everything around it, like a huge
magnet. You shouldn't go there. No one should
go ... It does not bring you anywhere ..." she said.

"So, in the final picture, I guess I am lying dead?
Rose is trying to get to me but the people around
her keep her away?" I prompt.

"No. There are no bodies. There is nothing left."
"So, emptiness must be left," I said.

"Not even emptiness. Nothing ..."

Anna stood up and came to me from behind. She tried to take
her empty cup, but I didn't let her have it.

"Time is up," she said.

"That's called cheating. You don't have to tell me
if you don't want to. Now please go back to your
seat," I said.

I poured the coffee into her cup and added a splash of almond milk to it.

"Here you go," I said, passing the cup back.

"You blocked some memories of yours. You chose not to remember. And still you let me speak about it. Why? Aren't you afraid to recall something terrible about yourself?" she asked.

"I am not afraid. Mostly because you keep saying only good things about me."

We laughed for a moment.

"Anna," I said, "whatever happened in the past, it's gone." "I don't think so."

"You don't think so because you can recall it any time. But you cannot change it."

She simply nodded in response, and I continued on.

"Yes, I chose not to remember some particular things since it was destroying my present. There is always a reason for everything, and I trust myself," I said.

"But it is trying to get your attention through the third part," she said.

I didn't understand what the third part was until I looked up at Anna. In an instant, I knew she was talking about herself.

"Where do you go? When you meditate, you leave the house," she said.

She was changing the topic, and I guessed she was talking about the island and my trips there.

"I call it 'the island.' That's what my sister called it. I go there and it balances me.

It fills me with energy," I said. "How do you pay for this energy?" "I don't pay," I said.

"No, you do. Everything must be paid," she replied.

"No, not everything."

"In this case, it will give you the bill at the end …" she said, before falling quiet for a moment. "Or perhaps, somehow, you have already paid."

Anna's words were said without any bad intention. She was sharing her true thoughts because she was open with me. But her words made me wonder if I had somehow paid already.

There was indeed something that I was doing on behalf of the island, but it was so simple that I never thought about it as a payment.

The island was an extremely powerful place. It could fill you up and make you balanced or, just as equally, it could blow you up. Not everyone could tolerate the amount of energy it could provide. Those who couldn't take it anymore had to be released from their suffering, which was my role now. One such visitor was already waiting for me in Hangzhou. That was why we had to leave the north. After Rose woke up, we started packing.

"Why are we going there?" – Anna said.

"You can stay in Beijing. We will be back soon. No more than three weeks," "No, that's fine. I will join you,"

I was about to leave the house. I had a few things to do before we left the capital. I kissed Rose and wished both women a nice time.

From the moment I stepped out the door, my head was instantly occupied with my destination for the day. I drove for an hour to get to one of the oldest Chinese tea houses in Beijing.

Gentle music whispered in my ear from the moment I began my approach to its entrance. The intricate carvings on the furniture told the story of a lifetime. The people there were like falling water. You could sit and watch them chatting, drinking and laughing for a thousand years and you would never get bored. Time was passing slowly, but I wasn't in a hurry.

I ordered a pot of rosemary tea and asked for two cups. Although I arrived on my own, I was waiting for someone to join me. Not in the traditional way, however. I had no idea who

I was waiting for or when they would arrive. Since the day before yesterday, I had a strong inner feeling that someone was looking for me and he was close by.

While waiting for my order, I mentally checked in on both women. Rose was wandering in the garden in a half-remembered dream, while Anna was exploring the borders of her powers. Their suitcases were empty and left behind. The picture in my head made me laugh.

A young waitress finally arrived with the teapot. She was just about to pour the tea when I raised my eyes to get a good look at her face. In an instant, I found myself dazed. It was my sister, who I hadn't seen for more than a year. I opened my mouth to greet her, but stopped myself just in time. It was a trick. No doubt, this was my sister's face and her slim body, but the creature that owned it was not her.

It took me a moment to realize what had just happened. I had been honored by a visit from a dragon. He came to me in my sister's body. He looked completely normal, but I knew that not everything was what it looked like.

The dragon took a seat in front of me and filled another cup with tea for himself. My excitement kept me from speaking for a while. I could leave him for a second and come back from the island refreshed and balanced, but it would be so impolite, almost rude. And, also, no one knows for sure all the powers they possess. I could not take that risk. Finally, I broke the silence between us.

"I met someone like you before," I said. "Each time you appear, something terrible is about to happen."

"It is called 'change.' Be more progressive," he replied, taking a sip of the tea. "You can call me Lawrence."

The dragon was aware that I would reveal the truth, but he still appeared to me in my sister's body with a single purpose: to make me feel safe and ready to trust him. This is how they think. It is not obvious to them that the most repulsive thing is the appearance of a lie before a person who possesses the truth. They are trying to behave like human beings, but it is not in their nature; it is partly against it.

The reason why one of them had arrived to find me turned out to be completely unexpected.

Recently, all of the dragons had disappeared. They cannot be killed by human perception, but they can be forbidden from coming back to Earth. There was a way to do that and someone had figured it out.

Since the beginning, dragons never left Earth. While the body apparently dies, they seem to come back through rebirth. Recently, something changed. Any dragon who died would never come back. Someone or something was keeping them away from this planet. They would lose their body, which was well suited to this environment, but they could not get a new one, and therefore, they could not re-enter Earth.

The tunnel they had always used to return to Earth was closed now. It had never been stable, but this time, it closed completely. Not from their world, from this one, and now that something or someone who did it must be here among the people of Earth. I found myself wondering what happened to the dragons who could not now enter Earth.

"They are part of the Big now. In the beginning, there were seven dragons on this planet. I cannot feel anyone anymore. I am looking for a way to open up the tunnel again and keep it stable, or to construct a new one. I know you are working on projects like that. That's why I am here," he explained.

His words hit me in a powerful way. It happened just as I predicted. *My* thought arrived in someone else's mind.

I took a sip of my tea and put the cup back on the table. I watched the dragon closely, almost stared at him, but he did not understand it.

Worlds had been destroyed and rebuilt since the first weapon was created. Creatures were murdered and avenged. It happened all the time in a matter of a circle, and as a rule, I tried to stay away from this merry-go-round. However, not this time.

Everything he told me broke my heart. I had always had a deep attachment to their kind. I admired them so much that I wanted them to be untouchable by anyone, including me. And I was afraid that I was the only one who truly understood the importance of their existence.

Dragons had been inhabiting Earth since the beginning and will exist long after everything is over. They are known as dragons because after they appeared in people's lives, everything transformed. In old times, it was war and therefore fire and deaths. This was where their demonizing image got its roots.

Their input in human history had always been underestimated—or even worse, misunderstood. Dragons protected the planet from scenarios like the end of the world or a final chapter. They also accelerated global events that were needed at that particular development stage of society. Their tool was so-called "coincidence." A universal excuse and hideout for sophisticated and complicated work.

Though they could embody anyone, it was only through fire, according to the legend, that they could show their true face. Although dragons often appeared as men, they were far from being one.

Meeting one of them was a sincere and authentic dream, one I never believed would come true. It turned out my genuine wish was enough to make it possible.

Once, I was lucky enough to identify one of them and get a good look at him. But I had never talked to any of them or been so close. Sitting there, I took a moment to enjoy the creature before me, but not for as long as I intended. Suddenly, the tea house split in half and distant parts of the island appeared on my left. It felt just like I was looking through broken glass. I blinked a few times, trying to get rid of delusion, but I did not succeed. I immediately went to the island, leaving my new friend on his own.

I stepped barefoot into the middle of the largest and most spacious temple in the entire universe. The walls were made of a material that did not exist on Earth. The ceiling was so high that space curved. I noticed a disturbing feeling in my temple, which meant that it was not sacred anymore. It was contaminated by the presence of a stranger.

"You are not supposed to be here," I said aloud.

It sounded like three people were talking at the same time. Here, I have multiple voices. I stood in the middle of the temple. I knew there were walls, but they were so far away that my eyes couldn't reach them, and still someone dared to hide.

"Reveal yourself," I insisted.

And then it happened. I saw a man just the same as myself, barefoot and in white clothes.

"Are your hands red when you are back on Earth?" He asked, looking confused. I suppose he did not intend to hide from me.

"Yes, they are," I lied. "Aren't we on Earth?"

"No, we aren't. We are far from home, much further than your mind would ever dare to go," he said.

The man turned to the right and I suddenly felt a salty breeze.

"It knows we are here. I have no time," he said, turning back to me. "This place is alive. You know that. It speaks to you. You told me your hands are red, so eventually, you are going to die. Your sister must be dead already. But for you, it is not too late. We can survive together."

I remained silent and he continued.

"Since you started visiting this place, haven't you noticed how the energy in your body has raised drastically? The human body simply cannot contain the amount of energy that this place provides. It destroys a body. It starts with the hands. They become red, just like your hands. Just like your sister's hands," he said.

My face did not reflect anything, but I wanted to know how he had found out about my sister and how he managed to get to *my* space on the island.

"I am looking for the man who figured out how to control it. He survived. He lives with energy floating in the body and prospers. No one knows his secret. I have to find him no matter what."

The man showed me his palms. They were as red as my sister's hands. With a heavy sigh, he continued.

"I want to live …" He did not get to finish his sentence because the island threw us apart, sending us back to Earth. I was, once again, sitting in the tea house, just as I had been before. The dragon had been pouring some tea just as I left. He asked if I needed anything else. I simply shook my head.

Then, a thought came to my mind: *"Find him. Now."*

I closed my eyes. I was trying to find the man from the island. He was nearby, and the deeper I went inside myself, the clearer and further I could see around me. I sensed the presence of him just a few miles from where I sat.

> "You'll come with me," I said, taking the dragon's hand as we left the tea house. It was almost twilight now and the street lanterns had been turned on. Crowds of people, young and old, were moving around.
>
> "Are you looking for someone?" the dragon asked.
> "Yes."
>
> "What does he look like?"
>
> "He is like a crystal full of energy. Too much energy."

The dragon rushed to the nearby lake.

> "There!" he pointed.

I quickly followed after him, but I was not even close to as fast as he was. In an instant, Lawrence had simply disappeared. I stopped and looked around. There was no sign of the dragon or the man. I closed my eyes and tried to feel at least one of them. I tried to concentrate, but the environment around me was too loud, so I left the street and moved closer to the benches just before the lake. One of them was occupied by two people. In one of the figures, I recognized my sister's body. I was about to get closer, but a thought hit my head like a bell: *"Stop."* The message came from Lawrence. He was now holding the man's hand while whispering something. I heard the man burst into tears. He covered his face with his palms and sobbed heavily, but the dragon did not stop talking. After a minute or two, the man stood up and bowed. He left the bench, walking away along the lake.

I waited until he became invisible and moved toward the bench. The moment I sat down, the dragon spoke.

"He will live if he stops going there. He promised
he will."

The man's story was trivial. He was desperate and in need, and this was when he had discovered "the city." He visited it twice a week, sometimes more than that. Soon, his life had drastically changed. The peace he longed for was found and supported by the city. But soon enough, the man faced the only disadvantage of the city: each visit to the place slowly but for surely destroyed his physical body. He had been found by another visitor of the place who was already dying and who was looking for a particular man. Everyone was looking for him because he was the one who managed to conquer its energy.

"Wilfred, how long have you been visiting that
place?" Lawrence asked. "Two years," I said.

Lawrence looked confused.

"Show me your hands," he said. I did what he asked.

"That's weird," he remarked.

"My hands look normal."

"That's what weird, Wilfred. You are the only one who has escaped the destiny of all people who have ever been in that city before."

"Island," I said. I did not intend to say it, but somehow "city" sounded wrong to me. "It appears differently for everyone. For me, it is an island."

"It doesn't matter. What matters is that energy from that place does not harm you; it nourishes you. The man was looking for someone who learned how to survive its harmful influence. And he succeeded. He found you, but you could not help him."

I disagreed. I could still release his pain.

"Wilfred," Lawrence said, looking into my eyes, just like a human being. "How do you do that? Why is it that this alien energy does not destroy your body?" "Tell me when you find out, because I don't know," I said. "No one can have something that does not, in some way, already belong to

them. If those people aren't ready, no matter what
they are given, it will destroy them."

Lawrence was concerned about my circumstances and the
situation itself. He wanted to know more, but I insisted that was
not relevant to the problem that he was facing, so we came back
to the issue of the tunnel.

"Do you have any idea who would be able to close
the tunnel, and, more importantly, the reason
behind everything that happened?" I asked.

Lawrence didn't know the motive of it, but since he was a
supreme creature among people, he found out something quite
useful. Before leaving Earth, one of the dragons managed to send
Lawrence a message. It told him that a creature had arrived on
Earth and its appearance had created a huge misbalance. The
creature's energy differed from that of the planet, so it had to be
destroyed by Earth. Our planet was supposed to kill it, but the
opposite happened. The waves this alien creature created began
to *change* everything around us, like an activated bomb, but one
that kills very slowly.

"Why did it arrive?" I asked.

Lawrence had no idea, but he believed the tunnel was closed
and the dragons were gone as a response to this misbalance.

"So, you must find it, whatever it is, and send it
back," he said.

"It's not that simple. Even the creature itself does not realize what it is." "How is that a problem?"

"How can I send it back if I don't know where it came from? The creature itself doesn't know where it came from," I said.

"I believe that the moment it leaves Earth and returns to its own reality, everything will find its way back, naturally, without anyone's input. The old tunnel will be open again, no matter what. But in case I fail ..." he started.

"...dragons must have their independent tunnel to return to Earth," I said, finishing his thought.

Regardless of the intruder in my temple, it was indeed a memorable evening. I recalled it from time to time, now already far from Beijing.

Anna, Rose and I left the capital the next morning. I wanted Anna to choose a house for us in the south, just like she did in Beijing. Unfortunately, she was not in the mood these days, so I arranged everything myself.

Hangzhou met us with its cloudy sky and Cantonese dialect. We stayed in a boutique hotel not far from the West Lake. I did not want anyone to bother us during our stay, so I booked the whole first floor with a kitchen and private garden.

Almost a week had passed since we had arrived, but I couldn't seem to take action any time I wanted. Instead, I had to wait for an invitation from outside.

The eighth day began with loud claps of thunder. It was about to pour with rain, but I had an itchy inner need to go outside. I did not tolerate humidity well, but this inner pressure in the form of thought required relief by the way of action. Otherwise, it would disturb me for the whole day. The good thing was that I was aware that this thought was not born in my head. Therefore, it did not belong to me. It arrived to guide my decisions on a physical level and introduce a new circle of events.

These and other thoughts would come to my mind all the time, but most of them were not mine. This was one of the many incomprehensible phenomena of this incarnation.

The only way to identify true thoughts from false ones was to be devoted to your true self. This was what I did, and this was how I managed to get so far. It is an approach that sets you free from energetic waste.

On the other hand, thoughts from the island were "marked." They were extremely powerful and not resistible. It made it easy to distinguish them from the rest. Just before I left the island, I received a message.

"Relieve the pain." That was it. The invitation.

No need to understand it. My part was to receive the message. The time and place always matched the appearance of the required participants.

I came back from the island, keeping the foreign thought deep down in my unconsciousness. I found myself in a room filled with light, traditional furniture and the scent of coffee. The sky, covered with clouds, was watching me through the window.

When I went to the kitchen, I found my beloved Rose putting food on the table. Egg tarts served with honey and jam and two pieces of matcha cake. Milk tea for her and just brewed coffee for me.

"Where is Anna?" I asked.

"She left for a couple of days. She will be back," Rose said, taking a seat in front of me, like an angel. A gentle, absent-minded creature.

Three hours from that moment, Lawrence would ask me to describe Rose and I would not be able to do it, simply because she was faceless. She was close to being transparent, like light from a lamp. She was the one who brought peace. Her body was made of marble and her soul … her soul was like moonlight.

The dragon listened carefully to my description, but something bothered him and his human face reflected that.

"Do you want to know the nature of your relationship with Rose? It's more than impressive," he asked genially in the hopes that I would want to know. But I didn't.

How we met or if we ever actually met did not matter to me. I did believe she was always around. I was about to see her tonight, but first, the accident in the park had to take place.

In China, you can find places called 亭子(ting zi: Chinese-style pavilion) in parks.

They are a place to rest. A place to hide from the rain or whatever is chasing you. It's an "island" located in the corner of the park, a dry place when it's raining outside. There is a wide branch where you can sit down and recharge. Here, you can rest calmly, wait for the rain to pass, and then move on.

I agreed to meet with Lawrence at one of these places. He had arrived in the city that morning, concerned. He was trying to connect with other dragons every single day, but because the tunnel was closed, nothing ever reached the other side—until today.

> "I've got another message. There is a woman here on Earth. She is not present, like you. She is wandering in a dream. She is the one who *reflects,* and she must be close to the one I am looking for."

It sounded like he was describing my Rose, so I told him about her. Lawrence listened carefully. He wanted to meet her face to face. I didn't mind the idea, so we agreed to have dinner together later that week.

Lawrence had become aware of something important and he couldn't wait to share it, but first, he had to make sure Rose was the one the dragons were talking about.

A path made of concrete stones led us to the heart of Taiziwan Park, where we were surrounded by a sea of vivid blossoms. Vermillion cherry trees encircled us, and we were ready to surrender. I took a deep inhale through my nose. This was how

I inhaled life, and I intended to enjoy each manifestation of it until I was gone.

We were about to have a short rest in the next pavilion. The drizzle quickly transformed into rain, so we picked up the pace to get to the shelter as fast as we could. A young woman with short brown hair was already sitting there with her eyes closed. I was the first to step into the pavilion and my intrusion had no influence on the woman's state.

Just as before, she kept her meditation going.

Silence, like a wedding veil, hung above the woman's head. It was an empty space that appeared from nowhere and needed to be filled quickly. A wild scream was not as scary as silence of this kind. Her calmness did not come from a peaceful state of mind, but from leashed tension that needed but one negligent push from outside to be released.

Lawrence stepped under onto the pavilion, following me. As he did, time, for the three of us, slowed down. The circle had been closed.

The woman opened her eyes and looked at my face. There was something inside her that was crushed. I felt an invisible wave emanate from her, like a breeze. She stood up and slowly pulled a gun from the pocket of her gray coat. I stepped back, shielding Lawrence, even though each of us was aware of who the target was.

Somewhere deep in my mind, I caught a whisper. *"Relieve my pain."*

That was exactly what they all wanted, and it was why I kept looking for the person. Former dwellers of the island wanted desperately to be relieved, and I was the final step on the way to their goal.

This woman was led to me by a chain of well-known events. First, she lost control and tried to get back to the island, tried to get what we all go there for, but it did not let her enter. She got irritated and tense. However, this lady before us did not stop at just being irritated. She reached the point where the air around her became charged. Now, she was on the edge. This is a known scenario, and only one man had ever managed to escape it. The one who was lucky enough to find me when Lawrence was around. The rest were doomed to get what they wanted.

I took a good look at the woman before me. She had a weapon, but I did not feel like I was in any particular danger. Her hands were burning red with multiple wounds, like she had put them into a fire a day before. The color had likely reached her shoulders by now, but her gray coat hid the true condition of her body. Although I had never seen her before, I could have sworn she looked at me with recognition.

"May I call you Lily?" I began. I chose it simply because it was my favorite name.

In truth, this was not the first time the island had asked me to perform my skills on its behalf, so to make the routine more amusing, I would name each of these women "Lily." I liked the sound of it, and I liked that the more of them that arrived to meet me, the bigger and more beautiful my bouquet became.

"I just want to live!" she screamed, bursting into tears before us. "You could help me! You could help all of them! Why do you do this to us?!" Her thoughts were a huge, matted string. "You will pay for what you are doing …"

"I do not pay for anything," I said simply.

A couple of young people passed by. One of them, a teenage girl, noticed the gun. She stopped suddenly, causing her friend to bump into her. They both looked directly at the gun. It would have been better if they hadn't stopped, but it was too late now.

One of them, the one with heavy earrings, shouted out to Lily.

"Please, don't do that!"

Lily looked at the girl, terrified. She was suddenly looking at her mother, who had died three years ago from pneumonia. For a second, she lost touch with what was real and what was a dream, and I knew that this was my chance to act.

The more misbalanced the inner state, the easier it is to gain control over the mind. It is like getting into a car without a driver. But the car was already moving, so I had to move fast. All in all, it was easy. She didn't mind my presence.

Of course, the teenage girl was not her mother, and when that fact finally reached her consciousness, the gun was already held by her own hand at her head. Comprehension of the price of her own mistake hit her so hard that I didn't believe she would ever recover. Not even a whisper came out. Her lips just slightly moved.

"I want ... I want to live ..." she mouthed.

There are some occasions in life that I would like to pause. I would like to freeze the moment so I can get closer and investigate everything around me before something inevitable takes place. When the sunset hidden in the horizon is already too late. When someone dies, the story is over, but the single moment before it absorbs everything that matters.

This woman looked lost, desperate and unusually attractive. If I had ever seen her face before, I would remember it. No doubt, she had been going to the island. She obviously had abnormal powers. The look in her wide eyes proved my point. She understood. She refused to admit it, but she knew she had already lost. And it made her an incredibly precious prey.

For all of this time, she was breathing rapidly, like a running rabbit. But the last inhale was the longest. The trigger was pulled. One single shot and she was gone.

I was standing close enough to have my face covered in tiny specks of blood. Not a muscle moved. I was as calm in that moment as I was paying for a bottle of water an hour ago.

The two teenage girls gasped, covering their mouths in shock. One of them instinctively stepped back, not knowing what to do next.

The moment Lily's empty body hit the ground, I turned to look at Lawrence. He looked at me as though nothing had happened. His demeanor was simply indifferent. As I noted before, dragons were far from being human, and the concept of good and bad was something childish in his eyes. What happened just then was not comprehensible for my friend. The woman was suffering, so I successfully set her free from it. It would have been all the same to him if I saved her or killed her. After all, she was relieved and she did not suffer anymore. This was all that mattered to my friend, and also that we would have dinner at 7 o'clock the next evening.

When I got back to the hotel, I found Rose sitting alone outside. It was still not too late to have a nice walk somewhere nearby. We could have dinner at a local restaurant; we could go anywhere except the place I actually wanted to go.

*How would the island appear to Rose?* I wondered.

I had been wondering about that since I discovered it. What season would it be? Would it be a room or a whole city for her? It could be anything. I liked to guess, but not to know.

The next morning began unexpectedly early. When I opened the front door, I found a tall blond man with blue eyes standing before me.

"I knew you were not sleeping, so I came," he said.
This was the way he greeted me.

"Of course, Lawrence. That is always the reason. Please, come in," I said.

Lawrence changed his appearance and forgot to tell me, but no matter how he looked, he was always the same Lawrence I knew.

The moment he saw my Rose, he was stunned. Lawrence looked at her but his vision went much deeper than the body. The dragon's face reflected the shining that came from Rose. She—or, more accurately, her *bright* past—was the source of it. The dragon could see her true, authentic form, which I could not.

"It happens so rarely that it can be classified as a miracle," Lawrence said, trying to figure out how deep the roots of her origin stretched in the history of all time.

Lawrence had arrived just a few minutes ago, at five in the morning. We certainly did not expect him so early, and judging by his appearance, I concluded that he did not expect to be so early either. But outer events pushed my dear friend to arrive as fast as he physically could. This morning promised to be special for all three of us.

Rose went to the kitchen to brew coffee and prepare an unusually early breakfast. I watched her movements from the sofa in the living room when Lawrence interrupted me.

"Don't you find it weird that you have no memories without Rose? How did you meet?" he asked.

"It doesn't matter. I don't remember when she appeared in my life. It happened so many years ago that I probably forgot."

"Millions of years, to be exact," he remarked, making me wonder.

Rose arrived into the room, her favorite silver tray in her hands with coffee and teapot on it. She placed it on the small table by the sofa and went back to the kitchen to prepare some food.

When she left, I turned my attention back to Lawrence.

"I don't understand what you are talking about," I said.

"Please, answer the question. Who is Rose?" he asked.

"You can ask her when she comes back. What's the point in asking me?" "She will not answer. But you will. Answer the question, Wilfred."

"I don't know, and I don't particularly care. She is the person who brings me peace in life," I said.

"She always did," Lawrence replied.

He took his cup and sat before me in the armchair. And then he began.

"I was wondering why you are able to resist the place. You are the only one who does not lose their mind from being there for so long. Your mental and physical condition are still perfect, which is abnormal considering that you are a human being. I was thinking about it since that first day ... the day we saw that poor guy who dared to come to you in the so-called "island" himself. Do you remember his anxious, scared face? It only took four months for him to get to that point in his life. Four short months. But what about you? You never seem to complain about anything. I thought you had to be hiding something from me, but then I realized. You simply don't remember. Your existence is here and now. But to finally see the full picture, we have to fill the gaps from your past.

He placed the cup back on Rose's silver tray. He had barely touched the coffee. There was a second wave of questions.

"Wilfred, could you please share your memories of before the island appeared in your life?"

I recalled the day the island invited me for the first time. I could clearly remember being in Beijing. It was morning, and I could not recognize my hands. I tried to recall what my life was like before that moment. A simple answer came to my mind.

"I was nothing," I said simply.

"Exactly," Lawrence said, nodding in agreement. "You just proved my thoughts correct."

"I still don't understand."

"There is only one way to be nothing, and that is to be everything. This is what you actually meant. You were everything or everywhere, however you want to see it. We are talking about the well-known state," he explained.

Rose came back into the room with a large plate of freshly made sandwiches. She asked if we needed anything else, so I asked her to stay with us. The sandwiches looked delicious but I wasn't hungry.

Lawrence waited until Rose took a seat next to me before he continued.

"The reason why you did not recognize your body on that first day was because you didn't have one. I mean, you hadn't had a human body before, Wilfred. The body you possess today wasn't originally yours. You have the memories of the man who owned this body before you. Not all of his memories—just those needed to survive. You were suddenly a man with a whole spectrum of human emotions, which you got under control very quickly," he explained.

"Who provided the body for me?" I asked. "Your island."

"Why would it do that? I have nothing to offer," I said.

"You don't have to offer anything; you just have to take what is already yours." "I don't like this conversation," I said, nervously.

Lawrence had delved somewhere deep inside of me, causing something that was hidden to show up, and it was an unpleasant sensation.

"Wilfred, I would like you to ask yourself: what *were* you? Before you were nothing, what was your nature?"

I got irritated by his probing and felt surprisingly ... vulnerable.

"I've seen something you cannot imagine," I said, my irritation obvious in the tone of my voice. "Your tricks with appearance change or mind-reading are nothing in comparison with what I can experience. You know what happens when a huge star dies? I know. I can see it. It can be reborn, or it can become a black hole that swallows planets like pancakes. Nothing can escape it. You can be the whole planet, the star—it doesn't matter. Once it has got you, there is no way back," I said.

"Just like it has got you," Lawrence remarked, finally and completely proving his point to himself about us. "Unlike people who simply accepted its energy, you could take it back."

"Do you mean to say that the energy from the island originally belonged to me?" I asked.

"It not only belonged to you, but you were brought here precisely so you could take it back," he said.

"No man can possess so much energy that it haunts him in his next life." "Indeed, but you were not a man," Lawrence said, pausing for a moment. "You were a planet."

Silence filled the air. Rose smiled and placed a kiss on my cheek, which I barely even noticed.

"A dying one," he quickly added. "Before, of course. Now you're doing great as a man. You're enjoying your own energy. Your so-called 'island' feeds you. It keeps you alive and protects you."

"Can you simplify that for me?" I said, feeling a little confused.

"When you were a planet, you were caught by a massive black hole. As a result, it destroyed you, as well as all the objects that depended on your gravity. That's how you lost your physical form as a planet. Therefore, you were nothing. But all your energy was supposed to go somewhere, and it finally got to the opposite side of the black hole," he said.

"The island ..." Rose whispered.

"The island or the white hole ... we are talking about the same phenomenon. It generates energy all the time, and this is its curse. The pain of it can only be relieved when it gives it all away," Lawrence said.

I looked over at Rose.

"What about Rose? Do you know what she was?"

"You tell me. Now that you remember enough, you can figure it out."

After all this time, recalling her true value was surprisingly painful. In an instant, my eyes filled with tears. I recalled her genuine beauty and it made me happy, so much so that it hurt.

"She is mine," I said.

"Wilfred, who is she?" Lawrence insisted, encouraging me to find the answer. "When I was a planet, she belonged to me," I said. The revelation was hard for me to process and my voice cracked. "She is the moon. My moon."

"Yes," he said, finally satisfied with my answer. "It explains why she is so attached to you and why you rely on her so much. It explains your abnormal connection to each other, which always played its role in your shared destiny."

Lawrence continued speaking, but I was done. It was too much for me. My emotional body was tearing me apart. I remembered the ocean. It was in a different time or different reality, I could not say. I remembered it and the living room disappeared.

I saw a young blond woman before me. She was wearing a white dress and was lying on a black rock, relaxed.

"How much time have we been sitting here?" I asked. I was sitting behind her, but I knew she could hear me.

"You don't remember, do you?" she responded, her voice was soft and comforting.

"When we arrived here?" I asked.

"Arrived?" she smiled. The sight of it was a remedy to any pain. "We never arrived here. We were *always* here. We are just playing with our surroundings."

I looked around, trying to separate reality from illusion. I heard seagulls far away in the distance or high above us in the sky. One of them flew very close to my head. Far away, I could make out the shape of a few people standing in a circle.

"Everything here is not real," I concluded.

"It depends," she said, reaching for my hand. "Finally, you *see* again. We have always been here, and we will never leave this place. Each time you realize that, I can't help but be amazed. Only you know the reason for everything. You could stop it any time, but you continue to play the game," she said.

"Wilfred!" Rose screamed.

I was absent for a few seconds. The beach I had just witnessed and my house could not exist at the same time. Eventually, I left the body behind, dropping it to the floor. When I opened my eyes, Rose was holding my hand and Lawrence was helping me back to the sofa. He propped up my head, trying to keep me conscious. His face was close enough that I could see my reflection in his eyes. The second Rose saw my eyes open, she left us to get some water.

I felt much better now that I was sitting. I had to say something to break the tension in the room, but I didn't do it in time. Lawrence did.

"Wilfred, there is a reason why I brought your past to your consciousness today. The creature who closed the tunnel must be extremely powerful or have a bright influence from the past, just like you and Rose. People have always been attracted to you. To your gravity, to be exact. You eventually lost it when you lost your planet form. But you know, human beings, for all their unbearable fragility, are super sensitive to things like that. They feel it, sense it, but they cannot explain it. You lost your gravity years ago now, but they can still sense the ghost of it. The presence of something bigger, even if it does not exist anymore. The fact that it existed in the past or will exist in the future is enough for them to identify it somehow.

"What's your point?" I asked.

"Huge objects, like you and this creature, will surely attract each other in the same lifetime. If it has not happened yet, I predict it will happen soon. I want you to pay close attention, and if something unusual happens, you must let me know."

"You are talking to a planet right now. Is that not unusual enough?" I laughed.

Lawrence didn't understand the joke, but who could blame him. He was a dragon. We gradually moved from the living room to the kitchen, the three of us facing the new day together. Lawrence and I talked for two more hours about the new tunnel, its exact destination, and the conditions we needed to bring it to life. After everything was clarified, he simply left, and the rest of the day passed quietly.

Rose and I got a message from Anna. She had flown to India as she had recently gotten a particularly bright memory from her past life, so she decided to check if the place she saw still existed. We wished her a safe trip and got ready to return to the capital on our own.

Despite her absence, Anna still managed to give Rose a nice surprise. When we got back to Beijing, we got the news that Rose had been accepted for a job at an art gallery. That was a beautiful change in our everyday routine.

Since Anna was away, no one bothered our apartment for a month. Her admirers let us have a rest until their precious Anna was back. If I were just a man, I would be pulled by Anna as much as the others, but according to Lawrence, I had a strong energetic support, and since we are equally huge from an energetic perspective ...

"We *attracted* each other," I whispered.

"What did you say?" Rose asked, confused by my random statement. We were having lunch in an Italian restaurant in Sanlitun, Beijing.

"Nothing, dear," I said as I touched her hand. "I just can't wait for Anna to come back home."

The next morning, when I dropped Rose off at her workplace, I did not leave immediately. I waited for Rose to take her lunch so I could keep her warm hand in mine for a little while longer. If we ever met again, there could be a reality where she had no hands, so I wanted to enjoy them now. Lawrence joined us. I could tell him what was about to happen, but I stopped myself. There was no reason to involve the last existing dragon.

Just before I left Rose in the company of Lawrence, I found a sweater in the car and gave it to Rose, just in case she felt cold.

"Or in case I miss you," she laughed.

On my way back to the house, I recalled Anna's voice. I wanted it to be sinister, but it was not and it never was.

When I got to the house, I waited outside for her. I knew she was close.

I looked through the window of the first floor. I had stood right there on the other side, looking out, so many times. Now, I was standing in the street looking inside of the house. Somewhere in the middle, I could see myself watching myself.

It looked like I was waiting for Anna to come back, to find out how much she knew about herself, and based on this knowledge, to do my best to persuade her to leave. This was what it looked like, but this was not what was really going on.

I wanted these thoughts to reach Rose because she would understand. I knew what was about to happen. Anna would leave only when her circle finally came to its end. This was why I was here. I was the reason she could not start from the beginning.

The lantern outside our house suddenly turned on. She was here.

"Good evening, Wilfred," she said.

"Good evening, Anna," I replied.

She looked relaxed, maybe even a bit sleepy. The dress she was wearing fit her perfectly and she was carrying a small blue purse. Her luggage stood next to her. I moved closer and picked it up.

"How was your trip?" I asked.

"It was …" She paused for a moment to choose the right words. "…not as I expected. I am happy to be back. Where is Rose?" "She is not coming tonight."

"I understand." She looked at me like the conversation had already happened.

"Do you know what I want to talk about?" I asked.

"I cannot be sure. Just tell me," she said, going to the door so her face could be scanned by the security system.

"I want you to go back home," I said.

"I am home." The door unlocked and Anna stepped inside.

"Your real home," I said, determined to make my point. "I want you to go back to your real home."

The moment I said it, Anna turned to face me, looking into my eyes in the same way my sister did before she took me to the island for the first time. But instead of touching me, Anna simply blinked, and that was enough. The lantern outside, the half-open door and the house itself, everything instantly disappeared. Black rocks and an endless ocean appeared before me. Anna's clothes changed from her blue dress to a black gown with two heavy bracelets on each of her wrists.

"I will go back when I decide it's time to go back," she said. "So, you realized for yourself. When did that happen?" I asked. The seawater touched our toes.

It was high tide, but accelerated one. The waves were coming in incredibly fast.

"It was one of those days when your past was so persistent, trying desperately to get my attention," she said.

"And you didn't complete the ritual at once. Why?"

"I was not sure this was the way. I didn't know enough."

"And now ... Do you know enough to set all us free?" I asked.

I tried to take a step but my legs didn't listen to me. It felt like gravity had become infinitely stronger, locking me in place where I stood. She didn't answer so I continued.

"Let me play my part. There is nothing better than to know that both of us are free to move forward," I said.

By now, the water had risen to my knees.

I wanted Anna to feel in charge. I wanted her to feel that whatever happened now would be right so I shouted:

"Who are you? Who am I talking to!?"

Anna's gown was soaked through and heavy. The black water had now reached her waistline and continued to rise at an alarming rate. She waited. Her answer was announced just as the water rose up to our necks, about to cover our faces.

"With no one," she said.

I was pulled underwater by a power I couldn't resist. The bottom of the ocean pulled my feet down. I tried to jump, stretching my hands upward, desperately trying to reach the surface of the water. It was, of course, all in vain. This body could not bear the lack of oxygen anymore, so as the water flooded its lungs, I left it behind. It was now an empty vessel on the ocean floor, gently swaying and drifting with the water's current.

Anna stepped forward effortlessly, approaching the lifeless vessel. The water had no power over her body. She could move in any direction she wanted. She looked calm, but nothing more.

# PART 2

# LAWRENCE

R ose was sprawled out across some pillows, reading Ancient Greek myths. The hierarchy of deities amused her more than she expected. She reached the part where she found out that Zeus, the king of all gods, was still not almighty.

> "How big do you need to be to become almighty
> if even the god of gods is not big enough?" she
> remarked.

Rose had found the book on one of the shelves in my apartment. Wilfred asked me to take care of her if he did not make it back on time.

Just as she was about to turn the page, she was struck by a sudden, unbearable pain—a deep, irresistible sadness. It ran through her body like an electric shock, causing her to let out an ear-piercing scream. I immediately ran from the kitchen to her, turned her on her back, and carefully put a pillow under her head.

"I have no control over it," she whispered. "Something terrible has happened."

I tried to leave her to fetch some warm water but she grabbed my wrist. She closed her eyes, allowing the tears to paint perfect wet lines down her cheeks.

"Lawrence, he is gone. I know he is gone," she said, slowly turning her head toward the window.

When dramatic events happen in life, people need to recharge. Otherwise, they lose their minds, so I waited. A minute or two passed before she began to come back to her senses.

"I want to be with Wilfred," she said.

"So, you know what to do, and you must hurry."

This was the first time I had ever seen her so sane and connected to her surroundings. It looked like she had finally mastered her body and was complete. Useless, since she had to leave Earth soon, but still a beautiful accomplishment.

Time and space had no influence on Rose and Wilfred's connection when they were on the same material level, but as soon as they were separated, it worked against them.

Wilfred did not become a planet after his physical death. That time was gone for both of them. However, they could still be together. Rose would have to join Wilfred and become nothing. She would need to do this until he could find a new physical form. Otherwise, the connection between them would be broken and the possibility of finding each other again would be unbearably low.

I kissed Rose's hand and left the room. I went downstairs, carefully closed the entrance door and left the house without making any noise.

Rose waited for a few minutes. She wanted to feel that she was completely alone. Then, she found Wilfred's woolen sweater and put it on. Ten minutes later, she was walking down the street wearing it, her cheeks still not completely dry. She got a taxi to a bridge in the south of the city. It had been designed by a Swedish architect in 2002 and was remarkable in its form. It was fitting that it was far ahead of its time. Rose had selected this bridge two years ago in case she ever needed a way out.

Wilfred was gone. Rose's trip was almost over. I recalled their shared story, and I felt grateful to have been the one to witness them together.

From the day these two met, no matter what planet or what form of life they took, they were always standing next to each other. To see them alive together was like watching a parade of planets.

But not even this amazed me the most. It was the variety of material worlds they were able to enter. Just before Wilfred reached the level of planets, he lived as a demon ruler of an ancient tribe. He received knowledge from stars and shared it with others. He could predict and avoid destructive cataclysms. He was the most powerful being on that planet but, at the same time, he was extremely humble. He was born as mortal but died being praised as a god. That was why he was granted the body of a planet. Rose was so close to him that he literally pulled her to himself, so in their next incarnation, she became his moon.

Nevertheless, after he had been destroyed, the privilege was taken away and he became a common man. Rose followed as well. I thought it was a terrible loss for both of them, but I was wrong. The life they shared here as human beings was a needed step back before they finally reached their highest levels.

When he had just arrived on Earth, he wasn't ready yet. He was weak, broken and left without his soulmate. He took some time to recharge himself with energy from the island. Now they were both ready to move forward.

In the south, when I made him acknowledge what I knew about Rose, he was overwhelmed—so much so that he left the living room and the planet. I followed him. The place he found himself in was his future with Rose. One of many possible futures. They had found bodies on another planet and they became gods.

Rose finally arrived at the bridge. She paid precisely what the driver asked for and stepped out of the car. Standing at the edge of the bridge, she scared herself by looking down at the fast-moving water beneath. She needed to calm down, so she recalled Wilfred's face. She almost heard him say something.

"When you open your eyes, you will see something bigger than you. Bigger than us."

Rose stepped from the bridge into space before her. I did not see her jump, but when it happened, I knew for sure that both of them had left Earth and would not be back. Their part was over and did not concern me anymore. However, what did take all of my attention was the woman standing behind me.

> "Hello, Anna," I said. I looked over my shoulder
> but there was no one there. Still, I know she heard
> my greeting.

She saw, heard and felt everything. Anabelle. Anita. Alina. Anna. How many names did she try out before she accepted the name we knew today?

You were spending time with Wilfred and Rose because you possess all of it. Wilfred tried to teach you how to cope with your *sadness*, but could he teach you anything new? I thought Rose was a transparent light, but I was wrong. You are, my dear, the dark matter of this story.

Why would such a powerful creature send herself to this precise place and moment? I didn't know, but I would find out soon.

"Anna, I would like to meet you," I said, sending the message in all four directions. Her answer arrived almost immediately. It was a destination, and it was far away. Anna suggested that we meet in the most dangerous place on Earth: in the center of a volcano. I politely refused. It did not matter to me where we met. I guessed she just wanted to set me on fire. She wanted to see my true, authentic dragon face.

As a compromise, we agreed to meet at the crater of a sleeping volcano, close to its edge but still outside of it. When I made my way to the top, she was already sitting on the stone in a lotus pose, watching whatever was happening behind the clouds.

"I should have guessed you were not a human being," I said, breaking the silence.

"Your existence is not provided by the laws."

"I disagree," she replied.

Here we were. Two dragons, face to face on the crater of a sleeping volcano. One of them was in his rightful place, the other had arrived from the future.

I was standing in the body of Wilfred's sister. Anna was standing in a body that had not even been born yet. Knowledge would clarify, but the more I knew, the more questions I had.

"Seven dragons for the planet. We are created complete, without the ability to breed. So, what is your origin, Anna?"

"My father was a dragon. My mother was a human being," she said. "As I mentioned before, we cannot breed," I said.

"I was not a beloved child, Lawrence. I was an experiment. I was never actually born," she responded.

It made sense and explained a lot about Anna, but still, the information she provided had nothing to do with why she arrived and when she was going to leave.

"I do not belong here. I came from the future. When you are part of the Big, there is no difference between the past, present and future. But in this state, right now, this information matters to you, Lawrence. I will leave Earth, don't worry. Just as soon as I complete the picture for you and explain everything that, for some reason, you could not comprehend by yourself," she said.

"How are you going to do that?" I asked.

"You touch me, and the picture is complete. Your part is to accept it. And as far as I am concerned, *we* are good," she said.

"What can I provide for you in return?" I asked.

"Nothing." Anna thought for a second. "No need."

Anna stood up from the stone, took off her gloves and reached out to touch my cheek.

This profound method of communication highlighted just how imperfect conversation can be. The moment the future and past met through a simple touch, the picture was completed, or at least as much as I was ready to see.

It turned out that Anna's presence here in the present, which appeared to be the past for her, was only possible because her body was not reachable by creatures of the present. Therefore, her actions had no noticeable impact. No matter what she did or didn't do, her behavior just supported a future that was already shaped.

Wilfred would leave Earth with Rose no matter what happened, but Anna played a part in it. She let me know that she was the one who drowned him, and it led me to one question.

"Why?" The answer came to me as an echo.
"Murderer."

It wasn't a secret to me that Wilfred killed because he could. It was not because the island was making him to do it. The island was simply encouraging something that already existed in Wilfred. Anna's human side got judgmental and it led her to kill. It made sense, but the real reason was hidden in much deeper waters.

"Anna, what brought you here after all?" I asked.

Anna took me to the recent past, where I found myself standing before the house in Beijing, watching Anna, Rose and Wilfred enjoy the spring sun. Anna and the couple felt unusually close to each other, which made her believe that there was some ancient connection between them.

"Have I ever met Rose and Wilfred before?" This was the question that popped up in Anna's mind and she took her time to find the answer.

Anna put me in her head so we could pay attention to Wilfred together. Something from his past was eager to be received. Anna let the information reach us, and we found ourselves at an event that took place many years ago, far away from our galaxy.

I stood in the center of a huge gathering, watching the demon that I believed possessed Wilfred's soul. He was standing on the hill, waiting for the second star to appear so he could begin a ritual. Rose was standing next to him, beautiful and dangerous as a snake. Their skin was dark-blue. They belonged to a race of demons. The language they spoke was forbidden because the vibrations it created affected their surroundings like radiation.

The ritual they were about to perform required a sacrifice: two lives must be taken before the third star rises. If everything was done on time, this ritual would create access to the particular aspect of knowledge that Wilfred was so eager to have.

A pregnant woman sat before them in chains. She was taken at night from another tribe of demons and brought here. She was aware of her destiny and did not try to escape.

"No need to make her suffer," Rose said. "Let's drown her. That's enough."

Wilfred agreed. He was already aware of how rituals worked. The woman was just energy that they were about to transfer. Nothing more.

The last image I captured was Anna's face being submerged in the water. Wilfred's hands around her neck. He held her tight and would not let her go until she stopped fighting. Two lives were taken at the same time in a cursed lake in the name of poison knowledge.

Anna was deeply affected by her own murder. She was carrying this forgotten part of her existence around like a wound. Unable to heal herself, she took a journey to Earth at the time when Wilfred was at his most vulnerable of *all* his lives. He was relatively alone and had no support, except for his own energy, which was provided by the island.

Sadness belonged to Anna, but she didn't realize what the source of it was. So, the meeting was arranged to set Wilfred free. He didn't understand what was keeping him there, and Anna needed to balance what had been unbalanced. And that's what she did.

Wilfred and Rose had left. As soon as Anna was done, she would also leave. She was allowed to start again. I was the last one in this chain. When I left, a new circle of events would arrive.

Anna decided she had showed enough. She took her hand away and slipped it back into her glove. I heard a quiet noise behind me and turned to find out what it was. When I looked back, Anna was gone.

Since she left, everything had gradually come back. The old tunnel was open again and I felt that my connection with the other six dragons had been restored. Three of them immediately got bodies in Europe, two of them in Africa, and the last one took a body in Asia.

Dragons do not have any other meaning in life but to accomplish their task, and my task to bring dragons back was complete. I knew I had to leave without delay, but I did not. Instead, I looked around. I was standing on a beautiful island called Iceland. It differed from any other place I had ever been on Earth, so I took a few more seconds before I joined the Big again.

# PART 3

# ANNA

can't explain how it felt, just like you cannot show me your blue and compare it with my blue. What happened to me was no one's fault. I had nothing; therefore, I lost nothing. Did it actually happen to me or had I always just carried it around in my head since the beginning? It does not matter.

But if I was talking to a friend, who I believed would try to understand, I would say these words:

"My dearest friend, I am deeply and inevitably sad. Maybe the universe is indeed not infinite, but my sadness is. No matter where I go, it always follows me. In crowds, where I finally feel released from my burden, I feel its physical presence. I feel the breath of it on my neck, but each time I turn back to face it, I see nothing.

No matter what I am doing, I cannot fully enjoy it. It feels like no matter how deep I inhale, there is never enough air."

"Don't let it happen to you," Wilfred's voice said, interrupting the flow of my thoughts.

"I know you are doing it again," he said.

"How do you always know?" I asked.

"A specific silence appears in the room when you are doing it. You *radiate* these waves," he replied. He could not have been more right.

Wilfred was trying to guess what I was, after all. He thought I was playing with Pandora's jar of disasters, opening and closing it. The jar would always be there, but I kept it open by choice, most of the time. He did not want me to get rid of it, but he wanted me to keep it closed. However, what he did not understand was that I was not a modern Pandora. I was the monster that lived in the jar.

"I am eager to show you something. I promise you will enjoy it more than anything," he said.

Whatever he intended to show me, I didn't mind.

"The bodies are staying here. Now you are going to lie down on the sofa, on your back, please, and wait for me there. I will be right back."

Wilfred rushed to the kitchen and took ice-cream out of the freezer. He put it in two gray bowls on the table to let it melt so our treat would be ready when we got back.
He lay down next to me.

"If you are ready, take my hand," he said.

I deeply inhaled and grasped his hand in mine. We immediately left Earth, but our bodies stayed on the sofa.

First, what happened to us was nothing. Yes, *nothing* can happen.

A second later, the deepest darkness that ever existed was gazing back into us. It seemed that any light that reached this point could not escape.

A huge sphere appeared before us and slowly began to diminish. Before I realized what was going on, it exploded. It came through everything. Wilfred and I were in the middle of an event. It was happening *through* us. Huge clouds gradually appeared around us.

What we saw was a magnificent view that divided existence into two periods: before and after. All of the suffering I had ever experienced was now justified by the opportunity to watch it. I sensed that there was something so indescribably big behind the scenes, but I could not comprehend what it could be.

After the explosion, the ball of light remained, but now it was spinning rapidly. It started pulsing, like the heart of a robot. As it rotated, bright beams cast a powerful light into the space around it, like a lighthouse. It appeared to blink on and off to a distant observer.

Something gently pulled us back, and we lost ourselves in the dense clouds.

I opened my eyes and found myself staring at the ceiling in our house. In response to the thoughts that were flying through my mind, the body reacted, although a few seconds late. My heart rate increased in response to the overwhelming excitement, my palms became sweaty, and my hands began to shake.

"Breathtaking," I whispered. "I have never been so excited. I won't be able to fall asleep tonight." I inhaled deeply and exhaled slowly, trying to calm myself down. "I am pleased you liked it," he said, looking satisfied.

"I want to say it. Aloud. It was the most beautiful and touching scene I have ever seen in my entire life," I gushed.

"Dear Anna," Wilfred said, as he carefully took my hand. "A star died just now. That is what you witnessed."

When he left the living room to fetch our treat, I had a thought that would stay unrevealed to Wilfred until the end.

"No. I witnessed a star being reborn."